YOO-HOO, LADYBIRD!

Mem Fox

illustrated by

Laura Ljungkvist

PENGUIN | VIKING

For Linda Candy and her loved ones
—M. F.

This one's for you, Ebba!
—L. L.

VIKING

Published by the Penguin Group
Penguin Group (Australia)
707 Collins Street, Melbourne, Victoria 3008, Australia
(a division of Pearson Australia Group Pty Ltd)
Penguin Group (USA) Inc.
375 Hudson Street, New York, New York 10014, USA
Penguin Group (Canada)
90 Eglinton Avenue East, Suite 700, Toronto, Canada ON M4P 2Y3
(a division of Pearson Penguin Canada Inc.)
Penguin Books Ltd
80 Strand, London WC2R 0RL England
Penguin Ireland
25 St Stephen's Green, Dublin 2, Ireland
(a division of Penguin Books Ltd)
Penguin Books India Pvt Ltd
11 Community Centre, Panchsheel Park, New Delhi – 110 017, India
Penguin Group (NZ)
67 Apollo Drive, Rosedale, Auckland 0632, New Zealand
(a division of Pearson New Zealand Ltd)
Penguin Books (South Africa) (Pty) Ltd, Rosebank Office Park, Block D,
181 Jan Smuts Avenue, Parktown North, Johannesburg, 2196, South Africa
Penguin (Beijing) Ltd
7F, Tower B, Jiaming Center, 27 East Third Ring Road North,
Chaoyang District, Beijing 100020, China

Penguin Books Ltd, Registered Offices: 80 Strand, London, WC2R 0RL, England

First published in Australia by Penguin Group (Australia), 2013

10 9 8 7 6 5 4 3 2 1

Cover and internal design by Lauren Rille © Beach Lane Books
Illustrations by Laura Ljungkvist
Printed and bound in China
National Library of Australia
Cataloguing-in-Publication data:

ISBN 978 0 670 07730 4

puffin.com.au

Ladybird *loves* to hide. 

Yoo-hoo,

Ladybird!

Where are you?

There you are . . .

afloat in the bath
with Duck and Giraffe!

Yoo-hoo,

Ladybird!

Where are you?

There you are . . .

SCHOOL BUS SCHOOL BUS SCHOOL BUS

tucked in a box
with Rabbit and Fox!

Yoo-hoo,

Ladybird!

Where are you?

There you are . . .

stuck on the stairs
with a couple of bears!

Yoo-hoo,

Ladybird!

Where are you?

There you are . . .

outside the house
with Chicken and Mouse!

Yoo-hoo,

Ladybird!

Where are you?

There you are . . .

SCHOOL BUS SCHOOL BUS SCHOOL BUS

up in the tree
with Bluebird and Bee!

Yoo-hoo,

Ladybird!

Where are you?

Ladybird?
Have you flown away?

Is our game over
for the rest of the day?

Where *are* you, Ladybird?

There you are!

Zooming around . . .

in your very own car!

MEM FOX is the author of many beloved picture books, including *Ten Little Fingers and Ten Little Toes*, *Hello Baby!*, *Let's Count Goats!*, and the bestselling modern classics *Where is the Green Sheep* and *Possum Magic*. She lives in Adelaide, Australia, where she loves playing hide-and-seek with her adorable grandson. Visit her at MemFox.net.

LAURA LJUNGKVIST has written and illustrated several acclaimed children's books, including *Pepi Sings a New Song* and the *Follow the Line* series. When she's not working on books, she enjoys working in her garden in Brooklyn, New York, where she often finds ladybirds hiding among the flowers. Visit her at LauraLjungkvist.com.

SCHOOL BUS SCHOOL BUS